Book design by Mary Beth Fiorentino.
Typeset in Myriad Tilt.
The illustrations in this book were rendered in watercolor.
Manufactured in Hong Kong.

Library of Congress Cataloging-in-Publication Data
Cutler, Rowan, 1966-
Stop this birthday! / by Rowan Cutler ; illustrated by Elizabeth McClellan.
p. cm.
Summary: Zephyr wishes for her birthday to occur every second,
but discovers that she may not really want that after all.
ISBN 0-8118-3765-3
[1. Birthdays—Fiction. 2. Wishes—Fiction.] I. McClellan, Elizabeth, 1961- ill.
II. Title.
PZ7.C994St 2005
[E]—dc22
2004002861

Distributed in Canada by Raincoast Books
9050 Shaughnessy Street, Vancouver, British Columbia V6P 6E5

10 9 8 7 6 5 4 3 2 1

Chronicle Books LLC
85 Second Street, San Francisco, California 94105

www.chroniclekids.com

STOP THIS BIRTHDAY!

by Rowan Cutler

illustrated by Elizabeth McClellan

chronicle books · san francisco

Tomorrow was Zephyr's birthday.
She couldn't wait.

She couldn't wait another hour
in the morning.

She couldn't wait another minute
in the afternoon.

And she couldn't wait another second at supper.

Zephyr didn't sleep a wink all night.

Finally the sun came up.
It was her birthday!
Zephyr put on her sparkly party dress!

The doorbell rang 10 times.
It was 10 of Zephyr's dearest friends.
She blew out the candles. She pinned the tail on the donkey.
She ate cake and ice cream. She got oh-so-many presents.

That night when Zephyr climbed into bed,
the Birthday Fairy came and asked,
"What is your wish, my darling?"
Zephyr said, "I wish it was my birthday every day!"

And the Birthday Fairy made it come true.

When Zephyr woke up
it was her birthday all over again.
She danced into her dress.
The doorbell rang 100 times. It was 100 of her dearest friends!
They all helped her blow out the candles.
Zephyr pinned two tails on the donkey.
She munched on a mountain of cake and ice cream.
She got oh-so-SO-many presents.

That night the Birthday Fairy came again.
And again she asked, "What is your wish, my darling?"
This time Zephyr answered,
"I want it to be my birthday every minute!"

And the Birthday Fairy made it come true.

Before Zephyr even put her head on the pillow
it was her birthday again! She yanked on her dress!
The doorbell rang 1,000 times. It was 1,000 of her dearest friends!
She flew past the candles! She slammed the tail on the donkey!
She gobbled her cake and ice cream!
She grabbed her so-so-SO-many presents!

One minute later,
the Birthday Fairy zoomed by
and speedily asked,
"What is your wish, my darling?"
Zephyr replied,
"I want it to be my birthday every second!"

And the Birthday Fairy made it come true.

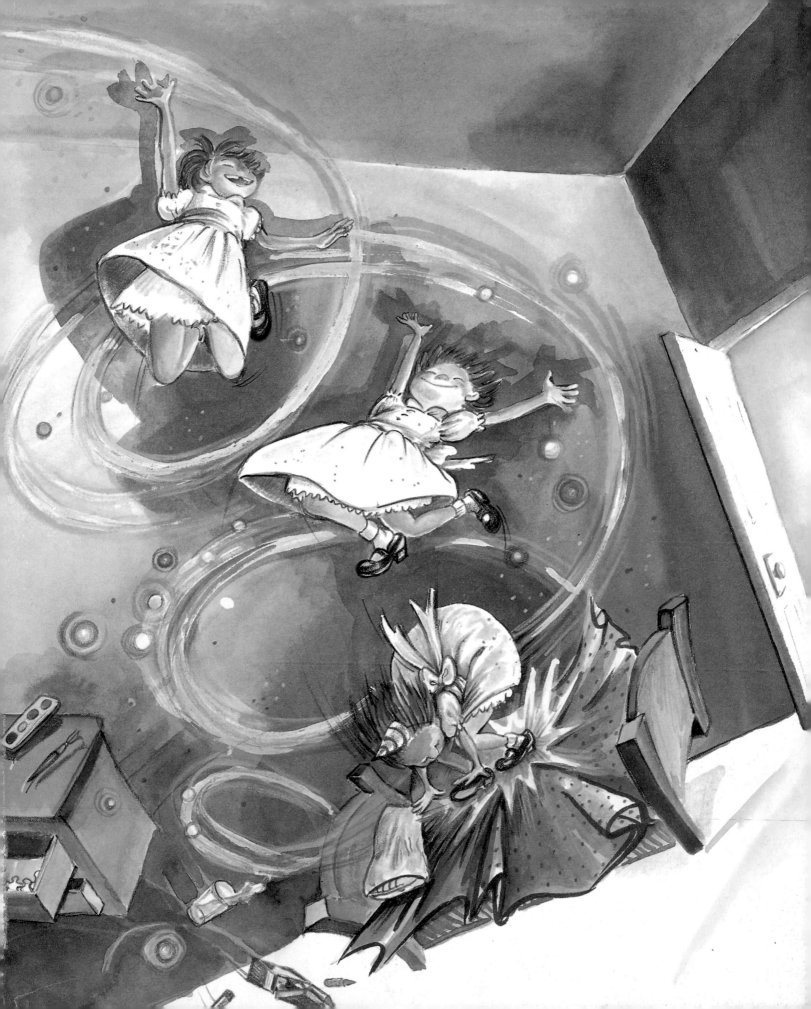

Before Zephyr could even blink
it was her birthday again!
The doorbell would not stop ringing!
She blew out the donkey!
She pinned the tail on the ice cream!
She tripped over the presents!

The next second it was Zephyr's birthday *again!*
Her dress got splooshed!
The front door cracked!
The cake sizzled!
The presents came tumbling down!
Finally Zephyr yelled,

And the Birthday Fairy made it come true.

Zephyr hung up her dress.
She mopped up the ice cream.
She gave the presents back and sent everybody home.

Then Zephyr climbed up to her tree fort.
Her face felt hot. The air was cool. She saw a shooting star.
"Next time," Zephyr said, "I want just one birthday."
"For that, you must wait a whole year," the Birthday Fairy replied.
"That's too long!" cried Zephyr.
"It's only 365 days," said the Birthday Fairy.

"Let's count stars while we wait."

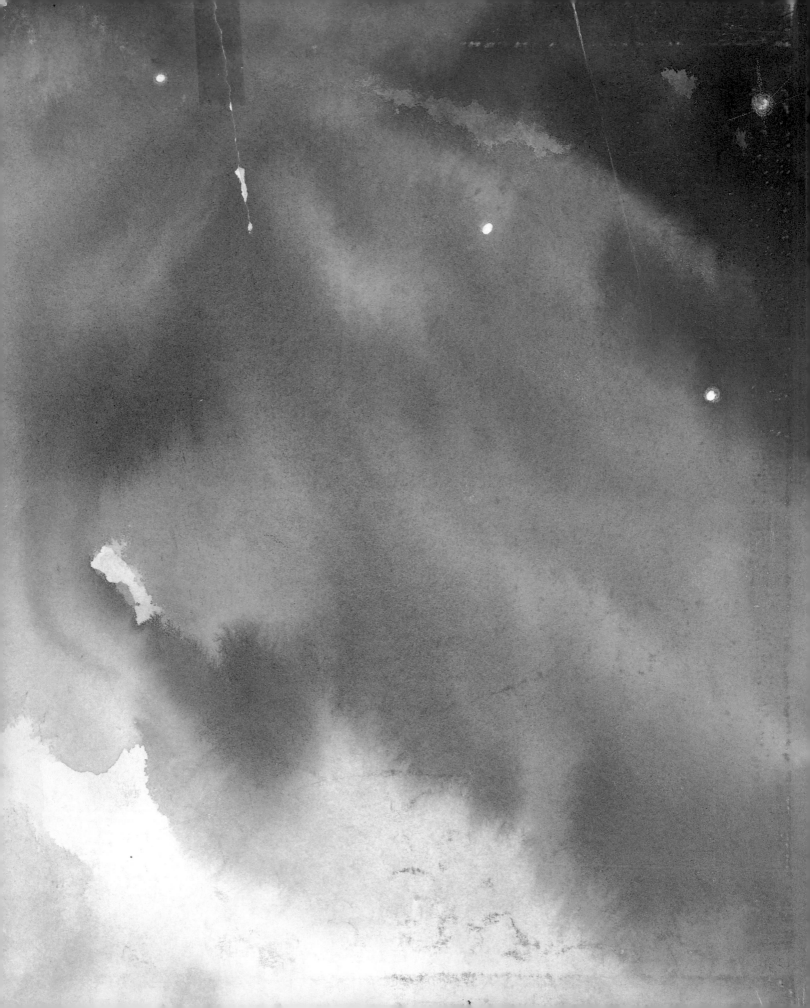